For all the little cubs
—R.d.S.

To my parents and Emily
—K.G.

Text copyright © 2024 by Randall de Sève • Jacket art and interior illustrations copyright © 2024 by Kate Gardiner
All rights reserved. Published in the United States by Random House Studio, an imprint of Random House Children's Books, a division of
Penguin Random House LLC, New York. • Random House Studio with colophon is a registered trademark of Penguin Random House LLC.
Visit us on the Web! rhcbooks.com • Educators and librarians, for a variety of teaching tools, visit us at RHTeachersLibrarians.com
Library of Congress Cataloging-in-Publication Data is available upon request. • ISBN 978-0-593-64549-9 (trade) —
ISBN 978-0-593-64550-5 (lib. bdg.) — ISBN 978-0-593-64551-2 (ebook) • The artist used gouache and colored pencils
to create the illustrations for this book. • The text of this book is set in 21-point Bembo Book MT Pro.
Interior design by Paula Baver • MANUFACTURED IN CHINA • 10 9 8 7 6 5 4 3 2 1 • First Edition

sometimes we fall

WRITTEN BY
randall de sève

ARTWORK BY
kate gardiner

RANDOM HOUSE STUDIO ⌂ NEW YORK

I't's a problem when you want a purple plum, too . . .

. . . but you're scared to leap.

"What if I try and I miss?" you ask.

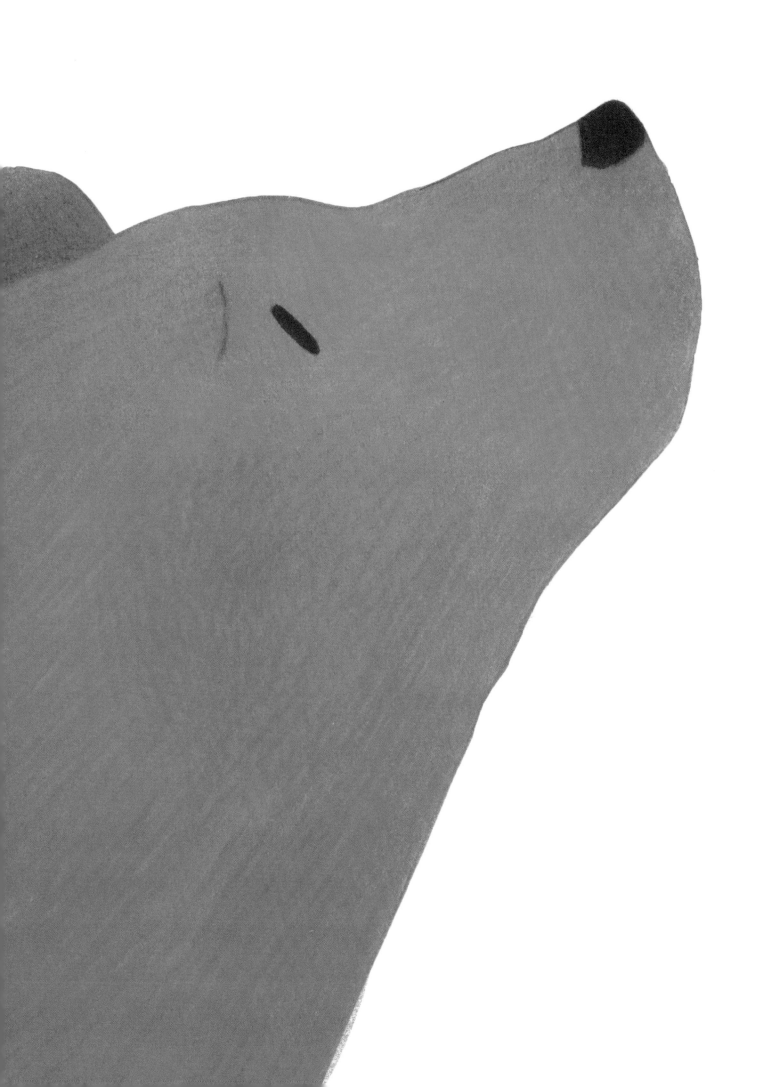

"Sometimes we try and we miss,"
your mama says, munching ripe purple fruit.
"It's okay."

It's a problem when you want a ripe purple plum, too, but you're scared to climb.

"What if it rains, and I grip and slip
and scratch my paws?" you ask.

"Sometimes we slip and scratch our paws," your mama says, munching juicy, ripe purple fruit.

"It's okay."

It's a problem when you want
a juicy, ripe purple plum, too,
but you're scared to scramble.
"What if a strong wind blows,
and the tree shakes, and I wobble
and bump my nose?" you ask.

"Sometimes we wobble and bump our noses,"
your mama says, munching sweet-smelling, juicy,
ripe purple fruit.
"It's okay."

It's a problem when you want a sweet-smelling, juicy, ripe purple plum, too, but you're scared to reach.

"What if, even though I'm a little cub, I'm way too big for the branch, and it breaks and *I FALL?*" you ask.

But now you also know the answer.

So you reach.

And you

fall.

Which happens sometimes.

And it's okay.

And sometimes it's even . . .

Delicious!